The Adventures of

SWAMP LILY

By
Ed Carlson

For information regarding permission, please write to: info@barringerpublishing.com

Copyright 2002 TXU-058-971
ED CARLSON

Barringer Publishing, Naples, Florida
www.barringerpublishing.com

Design and Layout by Linda S. Duider
Cape Coral, Florida

ISBN 978-1-954396-78-4
Library of Congress Cataloging-in-Publication Data
The Adventures of Swamp Lilly | Ed Carlson

Printed in U.S.A.

To Rudy and Ellen Carlson
who gave their teenager free
rein to explore the Glades.

Ed Carlson

Contents

Glades Wisdom

There is a culture of people who love the Everglades. They call themselves Gladesmen and Gladeswomen. The Gladesmen were not historically well organized. Today they have an organization promoting field trips and Glades culture. They know all the trails and the best places to camp and fish. I asked an old Gladesman why he loved the Glades so much. He replied that the Glades are his home.

"But you live in Homestead," I said, "why do you call the 'Glades' your home?"

He said, "Because your home is the place you want to be. When you are not there, you just want to get back to it.

"It is your home."

Well, I guess I am a Gladesman.

Ed Carlson

CHAPTER ONE

Gator Crossing

"Look, Grampy, there's another one! And it's a really big one! We've never seen so many alligators on the road before. What's going on?"

"Cold front last night, Lily. Warm pavement is a magnet for any reptile. Best time there is to hunt for snakes."

"Could we save that for another trip?

"Now, is this guy going to move?"

"How do you know he is a guy gator?"

"Because females don't get that big, he must be a bull."

"Yup, and this stubborn old bull is going to make me stop."

Grampy had to down shift and smash the brakes at the same time in order to slow quickly enough. His antique truck groaned and shook all over but that was typical for one of his emergency stops to avoid hitting wildlife. No one ever had to remind me to wear my seat belt when I was riding with Grampy. That gator stretched all the way across our side of the highway. Males this big can weigh as much as a thousand pounds and take down anything they want for dinner like deer, wild pigs, even bears! They are the very last link in the food chain. Grampy pretended to be rattled by this situation, but I knew he was enjoying every second.

We came to a stop about ten feet away from Godzilla and Grampy tried blasting him out of the way with the horn. No luck, that huge bull just lifted his long lumpy head, turned, and looked back at us through the windshield. Unlike other reptiles, gators have big brown luring eyes, kinda pretty in fact. It felt so strange to have this giant carnivore eyeing me. I wondered what I looked like inside his reptilian mind.

"Um . . . Grampy? Wild gators are supposed to be afraid of people, but this one is scaring ME!"

"They tend to get brave at this size, Lily, and he may have played this game before."

"Well, then maybe we should just back up and go around."

"Best we get him off the road before he causes an accident. Let's try getting closer and making more noise."

So Grampy let the truck roll forward slowly and along with honking, pounded his fist on the door and yelled "Move you big lazy overgrown lizard or I'll turn you into a speed bump!"

This was pretty fun to watch but also a great excuse for me to scream and beat on something, so I leaned out of my window and joined in.

"Move out of the way, you big hunk of reptile meat! Move, move!" *Yeah right,* I thought to myself, *you are really brave inside this truck!*

Must have been the combination of Grampy's bellowing and my piercing squeaks that got him going. That monster straightened out slowly, pushed his fat belly off the pavement with powerful stubby legs, and dragged his huge, lumbering tail to the other side of the road, where he gently lay down again.

"Well, Lily, you've seen a gator change lanes."

"Grampy, it's like going through a prehistoric gate."

"Guess he owns everything from here on. Just wish he would get off this road. Don't want to see him or anyone else get hurt."

Grampy doesn't talk a whole lot. He says most people miss the best things in life because they were gabbing instead of looking and listening. But a trip with him is never boring because he knows the greatest places, like this old road through the Big Cypress Swamp of Southwest Florida. The road itself is just straight and flat, but because of things like the dinosaur we just met, the ride is awesome!

Today is my fifteenth birthday and we are going on a camping trip in the Everglades. We'll canoe through the Ten Thousand Islands, to fish and camp on a little beach we know there. There is no place else like the Glades. It is the perfect blend of land and water. You can walk or canoe in the same place if you want. We like canoeing. There are more birds and fish and plants than you could ever hope to learn. And it's big! Seems like the trails have no end and you could just keep on going forever. And that could be a real problem. It's the easiest thing in the world to get lost paddling through 10,000 little islands.

We've done this trip lots of times and it's my favorite thing to do. Guess that's why Grampy calls me Swamp Lily sometimes. That's OK with me. I think swamp lilies are beautiful! I remember the first time I saw one. In the dark shady swamp where it grows, it looked like a bright burst of fireworks and light.

My parents don't really like camping. Their idea of being outdoors is playing golf back in Naples. I tried golfing with them a couple of times and it's not as fun as exploring the Everglades. Grampy doesn't play golf and says his swamp rat genes must have skipped a generation. He was a wildlife biologist before he retired and knows just about everything there is to know about the Glades. He looks kinda like Santa Claus except his hair and beard are gray. He's got a nice-looking face that folds back into a friendly smile. In fact, everything about him is big. He is really tall and has thick arms and legs and a big round chest. But his shoulders slope down from his neck instead of coming straight out like most other men. Sometimes when I see him stand up and walk, he looks just like a big bear up on his hind legs.

We make a real interesting pair because I'm just plain skinny. It doesn't bother me because I know I will fill out some day. Grampy says I'm like a new, whitetail fawn. Their legs are so long and thin compared to their bodies they look like they are walking around on stilts. I remind him that since I got his swamp rat genes, I might wind up being as big as a bear someday and he better watch out!

Right now, I'm just a harmless, little blonde-haired kid with freckles.

Grampy is acting different on this trip. He keeps glancing over at me while driving. It's kinda weird. I looked back and smiled the first few times but now I'm just ignoring his game and gazing out the window. He's also checking his watch, which he never does. Yup, something is up but it won't do any good to ask. When it comes to secrets, he is the biggest clam in the sea. Dynamite couldn't open him up. I'll just have to wait and see what happens.

As usual, we were cruising with the windows down to be as outdoors as possible. You need to wear a hat or tie your hair back on these trips, otherwise pulling the knots out later will make you cry. Grampy asked me if I ever noticed how many other vehicles drive with their windows open, so I started watching. Guess none do.

The cool air pouring over us smelled like fresh cypress needles, a scent like pine but much sweeter. There are many different kinds of trees here, but the cypress is my favorite. In spring and summer, you never saw a more beautiful soft green tree than cypress. Their leaves feel like silk and flow from graceful branches like a lime green fountain. In fall and winter, they turn gray, grow beards of Spanish moss and look like groups of old men standing around talking. Out here, the biggest cypress trees grow in narrow freshwater creeks we call strands. Cypress and deep water go together. But most of the land is covered by flat, shallow prairies that look kinda like the pictures I've seen of the plains of Africa.

Today, the strands of cypress are great, green hedges dividing up the wide prairies like stripes in a living patchwork quilt. Depending on the season these prairies are full of freshwater or fire. Floods and fires are just the natural way of life here. The prairies that hadn't burned recently were thick, golden, shaggy carpets. The burned ones had fine short grass, like an emerald mist floating just above the ground. Throughout the burned prairies, thousands of tall, white egrets stalked around gracefully for fish and frogs. So brightly white, they shone like diamonds scattered on green velvet. I really didn't care how long this trip would take. No, "are we there yet?" from me. Take your time, Grampy. I'm loving the ride.

CHAPTER TWO

Sawgrass City

We launch our canoe at a boat ramp in Sawgrass City where Grampy knows the owner and can leave his truck parked safely overnight.

"Grampy, why do you always laugh when you see the welcome sign for Sawgrass City?"

"Because there is no city here. The name is a joke."

"So, what would you call it?"

"How about Dredge Barf?"

"What the heck are you talking about?"

"Well, some rich guy bought this perfectly good mangrove swamp and couldn't leave well enough alone. He brought in a giant muck-sucking dredging machine that vacuumed up the swamp and spewed out a dry spot for a city. He got this land so cheap he figured he couldn't help but make another fortune here. Didn't work, there is no city, and it still looks like something a dredge barfed up to me. This place is best known for street flooding and mosquito bites. When kids who graduate from school here must leave to find a life, you know something is wrong. Everyone makes mistakes, Lily, and this place is a big one and just doesn't belong here. Old money bags should have just built the boat ramp and quit."

Grampy is really good at controlling his temper. The only thing I ever see him get angry about is greedy people. He told me that greed keeps people from thinking straight and he is tired of seeing the Everglades destroyed by greed for land and water. It has been going on his whole life and he doesn't see an end to it, no matter how much people complain. He says in the end the greedy people get control of the politicians and always get what they want. He thinks the only hope is to help them love nature almost as much as they do money and feed their greed by saving what's left of the Glades.

"Grampy, I love this little town, and I thought you did too. What about your favorite seafood restaurant?"

"OK, the boat ramp and the restaurant, but that's all!"

"And where are the fishermen who supply the restaurant going to live and dock their boats? And what about the cooks and that waitress you like so much? Don't they need homes?"

"OK, alright this is a wonderful city! I love it! A regular Paris in the swamp! Rome doesn't compare! You happy now?"

"Yup! And you were right about one thing."

"Oh, really, and what was that?"

"Everyone makes mistakes."

"Oh hush, We're here."

Another truck was just leaving the boat ramp after dropping off their canoe, so we were next! "Great timing, Swamp Lily!

"We will be in the water and out of here faster than a squid can squirt. You get the packs, and I'll grab the canoe."

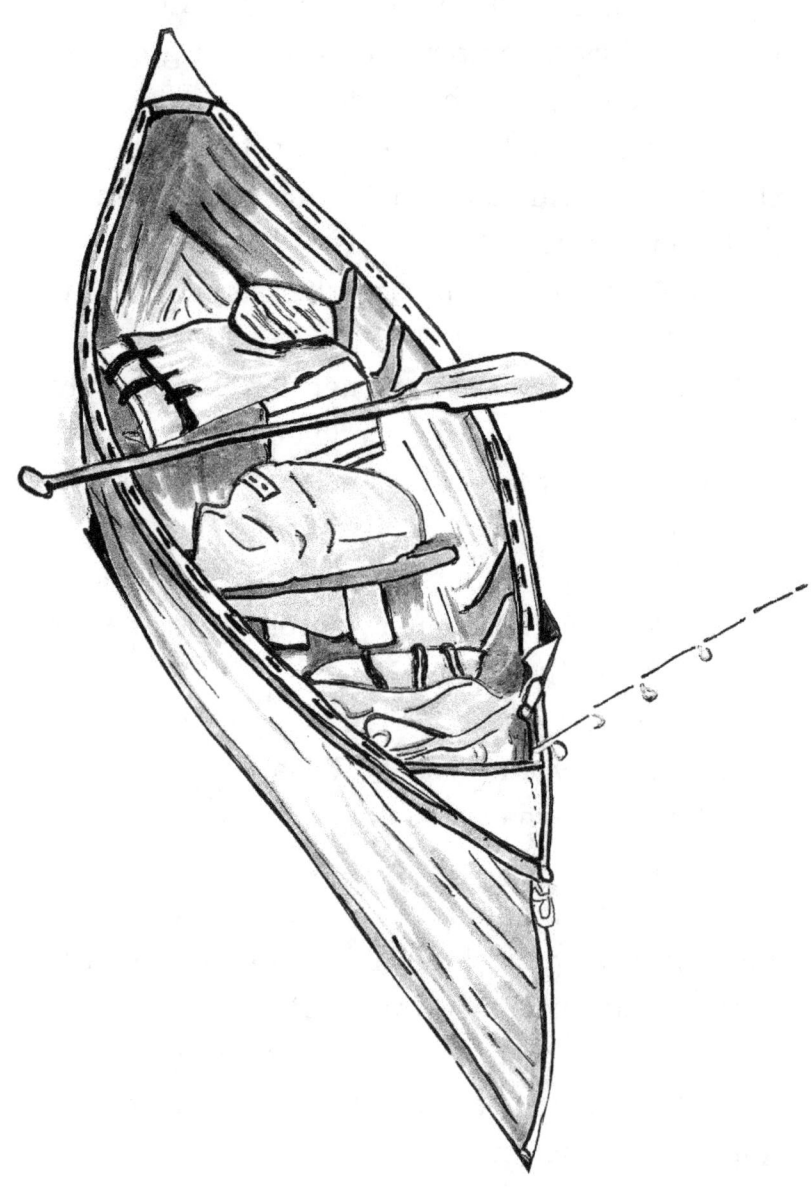

While Grampy was untying our canoe, I admired the brand new one that the other truck had just dropped off. It was dark blue and had fancy wood trim and woven seats. It was the most beautiful canoe I had ever seen.

Grampy loves his old aluminum canoe. He's had it for fifty years, since he was fifteen, the same age as me. It's all scratched and scraped from ramming oyster bars and who knows what else. It looks to me like it fell off his truck a couple of times and got run over. He calls it a floating book because the patches and dents all have stories. Says the canoe is like him, worn but not worn out. Figures it will last longer than he will so when he passes away to go ahead and bury him in it. If he goes to heaven, he hopes God will understand when he shows up at the gate with a canoe over his head. Says death is just a short portage to the other side.

But when he set that thing down on the ramp next to the new, shiny, blue one dropped off earlier, it really looked ridiculous. Where did those people go, anyway? It hurt to hold back the laughter, and a little snicker got out. Grampy stopped moving for a second when I did it, so I know he heard me. His beat-up old scow next to that brand new beauty was hilarious. I was still admiring it when he said:

"OK, we ready, Lily? Got your life vest on? Oh, by the way, get your crummy pack out of my beautiful canoe and put it in that blue one over there. It's yours. Happy Birthday! I had the outfitter deliver it for me. Neat surprise, huh?"

Spaaarong!! The trap was sprung and knocked the wind right out of me. I couldn't move or talk.

"What's wrong, Lily? You waiting for me to sing or something? OK, you don't need to say anything. But if you don't mind, we need to get going so we can catch high tide on the grass flats. I want sea trout for supper."

I finally managed to pull in a big breath and squeal, "Oh! Grampy! This is the most incredible, wonderful thing that's ever happened to me! I've just never had anything like this before. Thank you! Thank you! I can't believe this is mine!" I put my pack up in the bow and ran my hand all the way down the side. It was the smoothest, sleekest, boat ever.

Hugging Grampy is like hugging a horse. Getting around the middle is hopeless and the neck is out of reach. So, I just did it the usual way and raised my arms and fell against him. He wrapped me up and took me right off the ground. Held me there like a big rag doll.

"Lily, you're getting to the age when a lot of incredible things will be happening for you. Sometimes life might get a little complicated. Having your own canoe will be handy when you need to get away and think. Now, launch this baby and try her out. IF you don't mind being seen on the same river with me."

"Grampy, I couldn't possibly be prouder of you. Put me down and let's go! I'm going to call my new boat Blue!"

I pushed Blue as far into the water as I could before getting in. At first, I stood there trying to think of a way I could wipe my feet and not get a speck of dirt in her, but that didn't last long, and I hopped right in. I sat down and thought about how neat it was to be the first person to ever paddle this canoe.

The tide was starting to come in so that meant paddling against the current by myself. I've paddled alone plenty before. Grampy always let me practice with his canoe any time I wanted. He would say, "Heck, go ahead, what's a few more dents." But now, I felt nervous because this was all new. I didn't know how Blue would handle, and I didn't want to do something stupid and ruin the magic of this moment. All this thinking was taking time. I looked over at Grampy and he was staring straight at me, waiting for me to go first.

"Need an instruction manual, girl?"

That did it! I pushed off, dipped in full paddle and pulled hard. Blue and I shot into the river. I had to put my paddle back in fast and steer left to avoid crossing the whole channel.

"Wow! This is easy!"

"Yeah, I know the feeling, huge difference without a bunch of dead weight in your boat."

"OK, wise guy, if it's so easy, try to catch me."

CHAPTER THREE

Walking Trees

The trail was marked but I knew the way by heart and thought about how easily we learn pathways and places and never forget. After we spend a little time in a strange new place, it seems as familiar as home. It's amazing that some other critters are even better at finding their way than us. Sea turtles swim around the whole Atlantic Ocean and come back to nest on the same patch of beach in the Everglades where they hatched. Migrating birds and whales travel halfway round the world and back without maps.

And what about those incredible stories about stranded dogs and cats that make it home through completely unknown territory. How can they do that? Other creatures find their way without any help, and we are supposed to be the smart ones. Five minutes away from this familiar old trail and I would be totally confused. Maybe we forgot something when we got so smart.

Flat water is normal here in spring. The weather is usually perfect so windy cold fronts or thunderstorms are unlikely. This is the best time to come to the islands because of the calm water. My new boat is quiet and quick as some powerboats but without the nasty engine noise and smelly exhaust fumes. I love paddling in silence when my canoe makes the biggest waves in the river. I pulled for a solid hour before slowing down. It looked like Grampy was getting tired, so I stopped and faked a water break.

We were already deep into the Ten Thousand Islands, far from any sign of the great city of Sawgrass. This is a strange, mysterious world of small, weirdly shaped mangrove tree islands surrounded by green water that slips and slides in every direction. When the tide is moving fast the water swirls in great circles and boils up from the bottom. That's when canoeing gets downright sporty. It was hard for me to decide at first if this is land with water or water with land. Looking closely at mangrove trees helped me figure it out.

Mangroves are the strangest trees ever. They are green, bushy things with branches that grow all the way down to the high-water line. How trees can grow in salt water at all is really amazing. But for some reason, mangroves just don't seem as pretty to me as other trees. I figure it's because they are working hard on survival and don't have time to care about looks.

When the tide is up, a whole island could be one spreading treetop floating on the water. But when the tide goes down and you look closely you can see a zillion little trees standing up on their roots! They are all propped up on a bunch of skinny little legs. A mangrove island is a dense forest of spidery trees that look like they could take off walking at any time.

Grampy says they got their name from looking like a grove of men. Kind of eerie, but it's a very smart way to be out here because water flows right through them.

It's impossible for the current to get a grip, so they withstand the strongest tides, storms, and even hurricanes! Those roots are also a safe haven, nursery, and cafeteria for oysters, barnacles, shrimp, crabs, and baby fish of all kinds. Mangroves keep this whole place plumb full of life. I'd say it is basically water with trees and a tiny bit of land sprinkled on top.

It was still morning, and we were more than halfway to our campsite. We had never gone this far so early before. Guess I did get a little excited. The tide was ripping in and would not be fully high for several hours.

Grampy pulled up next to me and in a goofy British accent said, "My dear Swamp Lily, because of your impressive canoeing speed for the last hour we are way ahead of schedule. If you will allow me to take the lead, I think we have time to visit someplace very special."

"Sure, Grampy, but we've been through here many times. Why haven't you shown me before? And what's up with that accent?"

"Because, neither you nor the place was quite ready before, shall we go?"

"Grampy, sometimes I think you are possessed or something."

"Oh, don't be silly, just follow me, my dear. I only talk like this when I'm feeling rather proud of myself and a little pompous. Like your new boat?"

"You know I do and you really, really got me good. Where are we going?"

"Shush now and follow the master. Can your heart stand another surprise?"

"Yes, I'll survive."

Ed Carlson

CHAPTER FOUR

Sky Marsh

We took the usual trail a little farther and then steered left into a tiny channel just like a dozen others we had already passed. Grampy had to duck under mangrove branches and sometimes even pull himself through by hand. Then we were in a nice, little creek that was deep and not very curvy. We made great time and as we paddled east the mangroves got smaller and then disappeared entirely. Now we were paddling through a vast cord grass marsh with no trees or shrubs at all in front of either side. We went on quickly and easily for several more miles until this little creek just dried up.

"This is a major freshwater flow way in the wet season, Lily, but we can't canoe any farther this time of year. Let's pull our canoes up in the cord grass where they will be safe and continue on foot. It's just amazing that all this dry land is completely submerged by billions of little raindrops most of the year. Mind if we do a little walking?"

"No, I'd love to rest my arms and stretch my legs."

"It will be an easy walk. The Park Service did a superb, controlled burn here just a few weeks ago so this will be a pleasant stroll. Main reason I decided to bring you."

"OK, which way we goin'?"

"Skyward!"

"I knew better than to ask."

Looking up ahead, the marsh was misty green. Cord grass has round blades that grow back very thin and bright green after a burn. The whole marsh was soft and fuzzy looking. But if you looked straight down it was mostly black spongy soil littered with empty snail and crayfish shells.

"Did all these little guys die in the fire, Grampy?"

"Nope, they just died naturally. They thrive in here by the jillions until the water goes down. Beginning of the food chain for everything else that swims, crawls, or flies. No one notices or gives them credit, but the Glades wouldn't be nearly so entertaining without them. Right now, the rest of the population is burrowed down in the ground praying for rain and the opportunity to start breeding again. And believe me they will!"

"Just think of all this life in addition to everything back in the mangroves! It's fantastic!"

"Is this where someone needs to say, 'totally awesome, dude,' or am I just old fashioned? Lily, the Glades are a huge biological engine powered by clean water."

This was not a normal hike with Grampy. He usually wanted to go slowly and find things. Now he was covering as much ground as he could as quickly as possible. He was breathing hard and only seemed interested in more distance. He also hadn't said anything in a long time, a sure sign he was thinking.

Even though it was midday, the air was cool and lazy. In fact, it was dead calm, and the sky was completely empty. With clear air and no clouds, the sun could not have been brighter. We were the only things moving around for as far as I could see. Even the cord grass was standing perfectly still. On this soft, open ground, our footsteps were silent. When we did stop to look at something, like an old deer skeleton, the quiet was almost scary. Felt like we were the only two people in the whole world and the silence smothered us like a blanket. When we were not moving or talking, I could hear my ears ringing. After maybe two or three miles Grampy finally stopped, looked around and sat down on the ground.

"OK, Lily, this is it."

"Um . . . this is what?"

"This is what I wanted to show you."

"Grampy, are you alright? There's nothing here."

"You sure?"

"OK, I'll take a look."

He had either lost his mind or there was something very strange going on here.

I turned slowly around in a circle, looking high and low. We were in the middle of a gigantic marsh that seemed to stretch on forever. The sky was clear and quiet. I looked for something in the distance to focus on but there wasn't anything. The sky and the earth just blended.

It looked like the land and the air melted into a shimmering liquid. There was absolutely nothing anywhere between me and the sky. I couldn't judge distance anymore. I wasn't sure where to focus my eyes. I got a funny feeling, like being a little dizzy and floating.

"Grampy, this feels so strange, like I am more in the sky than on land. I'm standing on the ground but feel like I am up in the sky!"

"Me too, Lily, never felt closer to the sky anyplace else, even when I was on a mountain once."

"We are on the very top of the world and up in the sky here, aren't we?"

"Yes, since the earth is curved, you're really on top all the time. But there's just always something in the way that blocks your ability to sense it. These can be simple things like trees or buildings or hills. But out here, there isn't anything to get in the way of feeling like you are on top of the planet. The earth and the sky finally come together without any interference. So, who cares about Mount Everest, you can't get closer to the sky than this!"

"OK, Lily, enough of this nonsense, we have fish to catch."

As we were walking back to our boats, I asked Grampy how he ever found this place.

"Got lost in the islands many years ago. Wound up in this marsh and figured I would be better off just walking out rather than turning back into the mangroves and staying lost. I knew which way was north and that going in that direction would bring me out somewhere on the Tamiami Trail. So, I left the canoe, wandered out by land and had the 'sky' experience on the way. Eventually, made it to the road and thumbed my way to Sawgrass City.

"Next day, I called a retired gator poacher I knew and explained my situation. He was pretty confident he knew where I had been and would guide me back. Which he did without any problem. I recovered my beloved canoe and followed him out by water. He grew up here and knew this country better than anyone. In spite of the way he had made his living, I couldn't help but respect him for his incredible knowledge. He had very little fear of ever being caught with gator hides because he could disappear and reappear out of the islands anywhere and anytime he wanted. No ranger could find him. Would be kind of like me trying to find the stuff you hide in your room, Lily."

"Better believe it! Did he know of this place because of the sky?"

"Heck no, Lily, no money in that, he came here for the hides."

"How many times have you come back here since?"

"Once."

"Nice present, Grampy."

As always, the way back seemed shorter . . .

Ed Carlson

CHAPTER FIVE

Crocodile Research

We were in our canoes and cruising the main channel in less than two hours.

"The tide is finally falling, Lily, and the sea grass beds are just ahead. We made it! Time to relax and fish."

The right tide is key to fishing these waters. You want to be here when the sea trout and redfish leave their secret low tide havens to search for prey on these flats. Grampy put the fishing poles together and tied on his old faithful silver spoon lures. Then we stowed our paddles and drifted over the grass beds casting for trout. I hadn't retrieved my first cast when Grampy asked:

"Hear that, Lily?"

"Yes, Grampy, I hear jet skis. I hope they are going somewhere and not just joy riding."

"Going somewhere? Are you kidding, where would they be going out here?"

Two jet skis came flying through the islands straight at us. As usual, the bow spray, rooster tails and whining noises seemed completely out of place.

"OK, Lily, might as well reel in and stow your gear, fishing is over for now."

"Grampy, I won't do this again."

"Why not, Lily? You are only giving them the attention they want."

"Why do they act like that?"

"Been cooped up in Michigan too long, I guess. Aw, look, Lily, they are waving and will think you are stuck up if you don't wave back."

"NO!"

"OK, I will. Hi boys!"

"Grampy, this is too dangerous! The last time we encouraged guys like this to show off so they would run out of gas on their way back to the marina, the current took them down to Lost Man's River. If some passing fisherman hadn't found them, they would have floated all the way to Key West!"

"You're right, Lily, this is a very bad habit, and I promise to quit after these two. Now look, the first rider is putting his foot on the seat. He's going to stand up and do the ballet thing with the other leg. I say Bravo! Let's applaud."

"Grampy, No!"

"Lily, I would have some sympathy if these were kids like you, but they are fully grown adult males of the species. The other one is just jetting around in tight circles with his bow up. Sorry, thumbs down, seen it a million times before. But, oh my gosh, the ballet dancer has turned around and is driving his jet ski backwards! He is not even looking where he is going! Magnifico! Encore! More! More!"

"Grampy, I'm leaving. I just can't stand this any longer."

"Not so fast, Lily, they've stopped and are idling over to talk. Guess these two may have a lick of sense."

"Wow, Grampy, that first skier is really cute!"

"Jeez, Lily, a friendly smile is OK, but your gums are showing. Now, please just let me do the talking."

"Hello there, nice canoe! You two catching any fish?" queried northern skiing hunk.

"Kinda tough, because we're not fishing," Grampy replied.

"Well, what are you doing way out here?" continued hunk, exercising cute questioning brow furrows.

Crocodile research," Grampy replied with a straight face.

"Really? We knew there were alligators around here but not crocodiles," the second skier exclaims with an embarrassingly high-pitched voice.

"Yes, in fact this is the only place in the world where alligators and crocodiles live together," answers Grampy while doing his best beard stroking, scientific sage routine.

"How do you tell them apart?" asks squeaky.

Grampy seizes the moment, "Well, gators have that big wide mouth and can only chomp down and hold you under till you drown. Then they feed a few days later after you start falling apart. Crocs, however, have a long needle nose snout and can cut you clean in two with one snap. That's the basic difference."

"Well, umm, have you seen any crocs today?" asks wide-eyed hunk while looking around.

"Yes, largest one I've ever seen, big around as this canoe and longer, is lying right over there on that sandbar. Oops, well guess he must have slipped back into the water when he saw you coming. He's lying around under here somewhere," the master responds.

"Dave, let's go. This guy is making me nervous," chirps squeaky.

"Our research has also shown that crocs and gators live almost exclusively in these backwaters and rarely venture out into the open Gulf . . . which is that way," concludes Grampy, pointing with his chin and grinning.

"Thanks for the info. Have a good day, folks, we're out of here," says hunk while trying to catch squeaky, who has already left.

"Leaving so soon?" replies Grampy, before a double-handed belly laugh.

"Much better, Grampy."

"Yes, quite nicely done, don't you think? Bully for us! Shall we fish?"

"Why yes, I'd be delighted . . . ! Oh no, now you've got me doing it."

CHAPTER SIX

Fish Tales

"Fish on, Grampy!"

I knew it was a sea trout because they rise and break the surface as soon as they are hooked. These trout are not great fighters but a really big one can pull like a snook for a little while. They tend to school, so I was not surprised when Grampy was hooked up before I could get my fish in. You need to use a net with these fish because they have wicked teeth but a soft mouth and tend to fall off the hook if you try to lift them out of the water with the line. Lucky, I had the net in my boat.

Grampy taught me to take my time bringing in a fish. You not only land more fish that way but get to enjoy the excitement of the fight longer. This one was finally getting tired. No matter how many fish I catch, it is still a thrill to bring one in and get that first look. Yup, sea trout all right. He bobbed lazily at the end of my line while I slid the net under him.

"OK, mine is in, Grampy. I'll bring you the net.

"Definitely, Lily, this is a big one. I'll keep him in the water until you get here."

I handed the net to Grampy, and he slipped it under his tired trout with his left hand while keeping just the right tension on his bowed fishing rod with the other. I watched and wondered how many trout nettings it took to be that efficient and graceful.

"Five pounds at least, Swamp Lily, and a perfectly healthy, silvery beauty. No wonder they are God's favorite creatures."

"What did you say?"

"That these are God's favorite creatures."

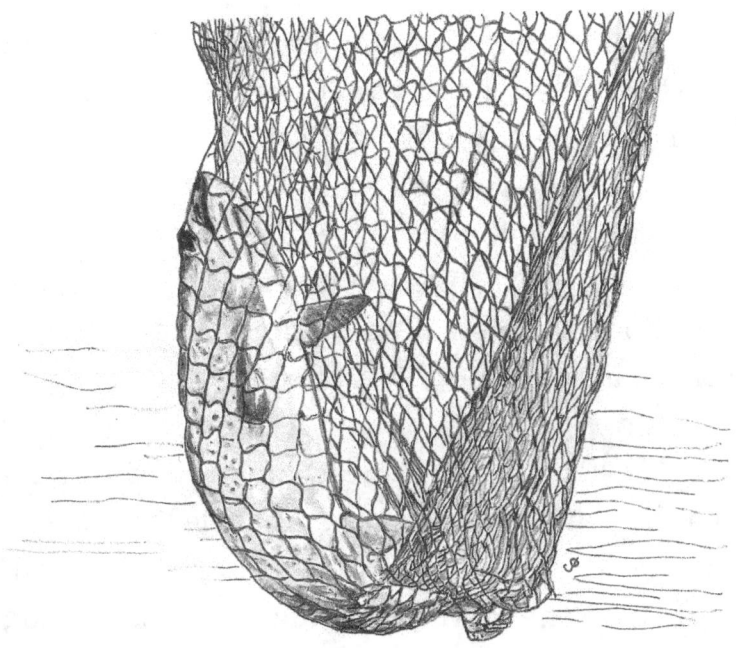

"Excuse me? God's favorite creatures? I thought we were God's favorites."

"No way, Lily! You never read the story of the big flood?"

"Uh . . . you mean Noah and the ark?"

"That's the one. You miss the part where God gets so thoroughly disgusted with people that He decides to wipe us off the face of the earth?"

"Well, I guess I remember that part."

"And He only spares one family on the whole planet just so they can build a big boat in order to save examples of all the land animals? Otherwise, there would have been total annihilation, and we would not be here talking today."

"OK, I guess that's true."

"Well, God could have done the job in any number of ways, like a huge meteor, or volcanic eruptions with lots of fire, brimstones, and even solar flares, but He chose a flood!"

"So?"

"So? Noah didn't need any aquariums on that boat. The fish and other marine life were all taken care of by God. In fact, during the flood, fish ruled the world! Imagine them swimming through the submerged cities and towns, going anywhere they pleased. Not to mention how delighted the carnivorous fish were with all the drowned people and livestock floating around."

"Don't you get it, Lily? God fed us to His fish! Not only that, when the flood was over, He still gave over two thirds of the planet to the fish. I'm telling you, Lily, God loves fish! And if we keep polluting the water, draining wetlands, overfishing the oceans, and generally disrespecting and abusing fish, do you know what is going to happen?"

"Surprise me, wise one."

"Feeding time again! And we will be nothing but fish food. So, you can release the rest of the fish you catch. We have enough for dinner. I'm done fishing and will just sit here and admire this beautiful creature. Thank you, God."

"Oh Grampy, now I understand, you have enlightened me, what shall we do? I don't want to be fish food!"

"Lily, please don't mock me. I had a serious talk with God and told Him if He ever needs another ark, I'm his man. I think we will be OK."

Sometimes with Grampy, the only thing to do is stop talking because you really don't want to know what else is going on in his mind. But he really did love and admire that fish.

I exercised several more trout and then we were off to camp. It wasn't much farther, so we would have plenty of daylight to set everything up.

Ed Carlson

CHAPTER SEVEN

Sea Cows!

It is so great when the harsh brightness of the Glades backs off in the late afternoon and you feel like you are paddling through some nice, innocent, northern water without sharks, riptides, and hungry dinosaurs. The water was calm, the light was soft, and we were gliding along happily until a huge mound of water rose below Blue and turned us over. Before I had time to get scared, I was underwater, wondering which way was up. Then I opened my eyes and saw a big dark shape coming at me. I screamed in a hopeless stream of little bubbles. I couldn't help it, now I was more scared than I had ever been in my life. Where was Grampy and what happened to Blue? Dear God, please get me out of here! I quit struggling and my life vest brought me up next to my floating paddle. I could hear Grampy coming toward me with deep, plunging paddle strokes. He had me by the arm in a heartbeat and ripped me out of the water and into his lap.

"You all right, Lily? Sure, took your time coming up."

"Sorry, but I didn't know the way. Think I'm OK, but I saw something really big down there."

"Look, Lily, we frightened a little herd of manatees."

I could see thick, dark, torpedo shapes of different sizes swimming around below us. The biggest were about eight feet long, the smallest about four. Harmless as guppies, we surprised them and one of the big ones knocked me over trying to get out of the way. Grampy grabbed my floating pack and put it in his canoe.

"We will take care of your canoe later. Don't worry, it's not damaged. Most important thing now, since you are OK, is to watch these guys. I love them."

Grampy was not disappointed. A big adult surfaced right next to our canoe. It blew its nose hard, spraying us in the process, and sucked in a new breath. He or she looked like a big, thick, whiskered walrus without tusks. Grampy mopped his face with his hand.

"Lily, was that great or what?"

"Are they like tropical walruses?"

"Heck no, aquatic elephants."

"Grampy, right now I am in no mood for jokes."

"I know, but trust me, this world is amazing. Their closest relatives are elephants. They are graceful little swimming elephants transformed by the sea."

The herd was calm now and we got to watch them for a long time as they quietly and peacefully glided through the backwaters like they have for millions of years. They are slow gentle vegetarians and got along just fine here in a world of big toothy predators until we came along. If they had trouble getting out of my way, no wonder they don't stand a chance against speeding boat propellers. Guess that transformed or not, this family of creatures is always in for terrible problems with people. Whether its farmers over in Africa or power boats in Florida, we just can't seem to find a way to stop killing them.

When they were gone, Grampy turned my canoe back over and miraculously emptied almost all of the water out in the process. Wet, and dripping, with a few weeds hanging off the struts, it didn't look new anymore. At first, I felt like crying but then realized we had been initiated into the world of the Everglades in a super spectacular way.

"Thanks, Grampy, what a great experience. Glad I am still alive."

"Lily, I can't stand any more excitement today. Let's go straight to camp. We should be there in twenty minutes."

CHAPTER EIGHT

Crescent Key

This is probably the best campsite in the whole world. A little crescent moon-shaped island with the points facing inland. The bay inside is deep and protected from wind and waves. You can paddle right into the moon and run your bow up onto a steep, sandy slope without a care.

From the bay it's just a few steps up into a shady forest of sea grapes and cabbage palms. They are really pretty together. The palms have long, straight trunks and stick their round, bushy, heads out of the top of the forest. The sea grapes grow in every direction and fill in all the spaces between the palms with big perfectly flat leaves. All the trees here are tall and there's lots of room to walk around underneath them without stooping. The sand is deep, soft and clean.

The top of the island is at least ten feet above sea level and unreachable by normal high tides. A few more steps west and you are on the beach with the shells and shorebirds, gazing out over the infinite Gulf of Mexico. Not even a hundred feet from bay to beach. This island is so small you hardly feel like you are on land, but it's all the land you need. We call it Crescent Key.

While Grampy sets up camp, my job is to find firewood, if there is any. We have a gas stove and could do without wood, but we prefer a real fire. The only fuel I am allowed to bring back is junk washed up on the beach. He would never burn natural driftwood, says its part of the island. Today was my lucky day. I found a whole wooden shipping pallet probably washed in all the way from Mexico. A big flat square thing made out of twenty boards nailed together. It was heavy but once I knocked all the sand out of it, I could drag it the whole way back to camp by myself.

Grampy set our packs in the shade and pulled out his hatchet. My pallet was knocked apart and chopped into a neat stack of firewood in minutes. Next was fish cleaning. Since we had wood, I knew he would simply gut, leave them whole, and bag them in salt and spices for roasting later. He always brought plastic bags with his own secret ingredients already inside.

Grampy never could figure out why people would come to the outdoors and hide in a tent. We drove a few stakes into the beach and set up our mosquito bars, one on each side of where our fire would be. They are like one-person tents made completely out of insect-proof netting. Later, we would slide our bedrolls inside and sleep in a natural world of stars and breezes. We keep a tent in case of rain. We also brought our folding camp chairs, which Grampy calls one of mankind's greatest inventions. He let me build the fire while he unpacked the grill. No big deal. I piled up some pallet pieces, sprayed on mineral spirits, struck a match and we were in business. He always said flint and steel are for boy scouts.

When the flames were low and steady, with lots of red, glowing coals, Grampy put the fish on the grill. They sizzled and sent clouds of delicious steam into the sky. He stood above the fire and swept the essence of grilling fish toward him.

"Ahh, Swamp Lily, food of the Gods! Get it?"

"Yeah, I get it, Noah."

Then he ripped a head of lettuce in half and doused it with his homemade "Ten Thousand Island" dressing. It was thick and red and had a luscious tangy flavor. Looked as good as it tasted on that dark green lettuce. Nibbling away on this salad, he turned the grilling fish, knowing the main course would be ready soon. He taught me that saltwater fish like these are safer to eat rare than freshwater ones because they are unlikely to have parasites that could make us sick. He always cooked freshwater fish hard.

We used paper plates and ate with our fingers as much as possible. We needed forks to peel the trout meat away from the hot sticky skin and bones, but my gosh, you've never had a better meal than those fresh sea trout and that rich crunchy salad. Sea trout are so light and fresh they actually taste sweet, not oily and strong like some other fish I've had.

Then we burned our plates and leftovers in the fire and went wading. The Gulf was unusually cold and muddy. Grampy thought it must have been stirred up by some distant storm. The water felt good, but the campsite looked more inviting, so we climbed back out, dried off, changed clothes, and piled more wood on the fire. Grampy always made me a little dressing room back in the sea grapes with a tarp. Rule was I stayed in there till he gave the signal he was finished dressing outside. It felt so good to be bathed, in clean clothes, full of good food and really, really tired.

We sat together on the beach in our chairs facing the sunset like a couple of movie directors. Not much action on this set, everything was so calm. The air still wasn't moving, and the Gulf looked frozen. I could hear the tiniest sounds, like small fish slurping bugs off the surface of the bay and a little prairie warbler pecking her way through the palm fronds for one last caterpillar before bed. The sky was deep, dark red at the horizon and turned purple as you looked up. Stars were beginning to light up behind us.

"Lily, ever seen the green flash when the sun sets in the Gulf?"

"No, must be color blind, I guess."

"Me too. You handled your canoe beautifully today. I could see your pride in the straightness of your back and the power of your strokes. Just a fact, I am not fishing for compliments."

"Just did what you taught me."

"Thanks, Lily, I'm proud of you and I'm really tired. Mind if I climb into my mosquito bar? We can talk by the fire, but I want to lie down."

"Heck no, Grampy, I was thinking about crawling in too. Been a lot of excitement for this kid today. Without a doubt the best birthday ever for me and I am exhausted too."

"That's great to hear, Lily, I just thought I was getting old."

We relaxed in our mosquito bars. Grampy adjusted the sand under his bedroll to fit his hips and shoulders. I just sat inside mine facing the fire.

"Grampy, people think it's really neat that you are old. They talk about how young you are for your age."

"Guess they can't think of anything better to waste their time talking about, Lily."

"Well maybe they admire your age and want to learn the secret of living a very long time."

"Oh, so they have selfish motives!"

"Selfish or not, I want to know the secret too. And how you learned it!"

"Is that all?"

"Yes, for now."

"Are you going to tell anyone else?"

"I promise not to tell anyone."

"Have you ever managed to do that before?"

"No, but I am going to start now."

"Excellent, just for being honest I will tell you the secret."

"Thank you Grampy, I am ready! Impart your wisdom!"

CHAPTER NINE

Campfire Secrets

Little one, this is scary to learn, but the secret is that there is no secret. No one is in complete control of their life. Just about anything can happen at any time. We can only control the little stuff like what we eat or wear. Old people are just smart about how they live and avoid dangerous situations, but the rest is just luck and good, God-given genetics. If you don't get caught in an accident or sprout a cancer, you are just plain lucky. That's really why people appreciate old age. It's like winning the lottery."

"You're kidding. That's it?"

"You were looking for something more profound?"

"Well heck, yeah! Like some secret formula or hidden knowledge."

"Like on the Sci-Fi Channel?"

"Sorry, Grampy, but there has got to be more to it. You make life sound so cold and careless."

"All right then, you win. You finally dragged it out of me. There really is a secret to living a very, very long time. Sure, you want to know?"

"Yes, get on with it and quit teasing me! There's nothing better that a good secret!"

"Not even fire-baked marshmallows smushed in chocolate bars?"

"Just tell me!"

"Well, Swamp Lily, you can always fall in love with someone who doesn't love you. And long for them foolishly for the rest of your life. Then no matter how long you live it will seem like an eternity."

"Grampy . . . ! You're not kidding, are you . . . ? And you're not talking about Grammy either."

"No, this was before Grammy."

"Oh my God, this is the biggest secret I've ever heard! Wow, this is huge, gigantic! No one has ever talked to me like this before! Thank you so much! I love you and feel closer to you now more than ever. We've like, bonded! You ARE trying to give me a heart attack on my birthday, aren't you? I don't know what to say!"

"Now, that's different."

For a little while, we both just watched the fire. I wrapped my arms around my legs and pulled until my chin was perched on my knees. I knew there was no pressure to say anything and never would be. Just not the way it's done around here. No one is expected to talk and shouldn't anyway unless they have a reason.

Study the fire, I told myself, *Take your time, and try to think of something to say.*

Watching the fire burn calmly, I really did feel different. Kinda like the way I do after making it through something complicated for the first time, knowing it will be easier the next time. Maybe that's what growing up is, having one experience after another, getting through them and building confidence as you go. You can't determine when when things happen and you just have to wait for them. So, that's why it takes so long to grow up! Holy cow, no wonder Grampy is so confident!

"Grampy, I think I'm feeling a little older."

"Sneaks right up on you, doesn't it?"

"Wait a minute . . . I'VE GOT IT! Does she know?"

"Which one?"

"Oh Lord! Any of them! You are making me crazy!"

"Yup, they know. Your Grammy knew before we married that if I'd had my way things would have turned out differently. But she also knows I love her and will always be faithful to her. Lily, you can't choose who you fall in love with, and you can't convince others to love you if they just don't. Might as well learn those lessons right now."

"Do you know where she is?"

"Yes, I still do after all these years."

"Grampy, you didn't have to tell me this, why did you?"

"Because it's time you started to learn about love. It's an overwhelming part of life, and not covered in textbooks. I know it's a hard thing to talk about with your parents. So, I put it in my job description."

"And you still think about your first love?"

"Yup, can't help it."

"Then I say you just taught me love is cruel and mean and painful."

"Don't forget wonderful."

"Then it's totally crazy."

"Oh, dear Lily, you are absolutely right, and it is much more. It is everything, love is the greatest teacher of all! But be ready, the lessons can be rough. Sometimes even causing people to do terrible things they regret later. The really crazy part is that if you open yourself up to love then a certain amount of loneliness comes along with it. We can't always be with those we love."

"Grampy, are you telling me you still miss her?"

"Not all the time, but I never know when some little reminder is going to sneak up unexpectedly. Just another part of my life I can't control. Sometimes, I think it actually helps me appreciate life more."

"Does everyone fall in love like that?"

"I don't know, but I think my life is pretty typical. Maybe others do and just don't admit to it."

"Grampy, how do you know when you are in love?"

"One real good measure is how big a fool you make out of yourself for someone."

"Oh yeah, I already know. We learn that really young. When a boy starts acting silly around you it's a sure sign he likes you."

"Yup, and if he gets to the poetry writing stage, he's a real goner."

"But I think it would be really cool for someone to be lonely for me and miss me."

"Oh, it's great fun until you're the one doing the missing."

"But I don't miss anyone like you do."

"Then you are not in love yet."

"Well then, when will it happen?"

"No one on this earth knows. But believe me when it does happen it will be spontaneous and completely natural. No planning or training required."

"I've seen some other girls kissing boys but I'm not ready to do that yet."

"Lily, there's no need to rush. Just take your time and wait until you are ready. You will be much happier that way."

"Grampy, when was your first kiss? How did it happen?"

"So long ago, I'm not sure about the first one. But I do remember a certain one like it was last night."

"Now this sounds interesting! Tell me! Tell me!"

"You want the whole story or the condensed version?"

"I've got all night!"

CHAPTER TEN

Hunter's Paradise

Grampy propped himself up on his elbow and looked at me with eyes shining brightly with firelight. He pulled on his beard for a few moments and hummed to himself quietly. I knew he was composing what would be, for him, an epic tale. Then he cleared his throat and began.

"I was nineteen years old, single, and free as a fork-tailed sky hawk. I took some time off college around the Christmas holidays to camp in the Cypress country and clear my head of all the junk being jammed into it. Lily, I don't care what anyone says, unless you are going to be a nuclear physicist or something you will never use calculus or trigonometry in your whole life.

"One day I decided to make a trip to Corkscrew Swamp and visit my friend Buck Johnston. He and I worked construction together in the summers. Buck and his family were real pioneers, living out in the woods by themselves. They always enjoyed visitors, especially me with my stories about the dumb things people had to do to get a college education. They lived in a completely different world of hard labor and life on the land, but they were very happy."

"Grampy, did they do stuff like grow their own food?"

"Most of it. They had lots of chickens, a few pigs, and a huge garden. The things they grew didn't require much care at all. I never saw them use pesticides or artificial fertilizer. A little chicken manure worked wonders. They grew several kinds of squash, pole beans, sweet potatoes, and big leafy mustard and collard greens. They didn't care at all about a few bugs in the garden. It always produced more than enough for everyone.

"Buck also had a cane patch. His prized possession was an antique sugar cane press he had restored. It sat proudly right in the middle of his front yard. A big, long, wooden pole stuck out of the side of it. Horses and mules were originally used to turn the thing by plodding around in circles. Buck used a little cub tractor. When it was cane squeezing time, he didn't need to ask for help, his kids would fight over who was going to drive the tractor.

"Buck was proud of his cane press and wouldn't let anyone else feed stalks into it. He also had a huge cast iron cauldron to boil the squeezings in. It was at least five feet in diameter but really shallow. All that surface area helped boil the water out of the cane juice faster. He built a nice, natural, stone fireplace under it and used what he called lightered knots for fuel. That wood was heavy as lead and got its name from the fire it produces. Nothing burns hotter than that old, rock-hard, heart pine.

"I helped him make syrup a few times and will never forget the thick sweet aroma of boiling syrup mixed with black pine smoke. Standing there in the woods, stirring that cauldron with a spoon nearly as big as a canoe paddle, I would not have been a bit surprised to see Davy Crockett or Daniel Boone ride in to say hello. There was a jar of that syrup and a basket of fresh baked corn bread on the table at every meal. They ate lots of vegetables from the garden and a very modest amount of meat. Guess the diet worked. All the Johnstons seemed to be in perpetual motion and had bright sparkly, eyes.

"They called lunch, dinner and dinner, supper, so I had supper with them, and Buck reminded me that it was New Year's Eve. Said the locals were going to gather down at Hunter's Paradise. I was just the excuse he needed to get out of the house and do a little celebrating. His wife, Judith, gave an approving nod in my honor."

"Excuse me, Grampy, but you been kissed yet?"

"Patience, Lily, I'm getting there. You asked for the whole story."

Grampy took a swig of water from his canteen and said, "Guess I am going on a bit. You still want to hear this story?"

"Absolutely! And I promise not to interrupt again."

"The Hunter's Paradise was a homely little place that sat all alone on the side of Immokalee

Road, ten miles from the nearest sign of anything human. There was just no logical explanation for its location or existence. It was built out of rough sawn lumber that nobody ever bothered to paint, and drinking seemed to be part of the architecture since the whole building leaned to the west. Pretty standard little beer joint otherwise. It had one big room with booths and tables along three walls, bar with stools along the other and a pool table in the middle.

"The only real décor was up on the ceiling. An old gill net was nailed up there and filled with parts and pieces of rare and endangered species taken from the Glades. There were shells and skulls of several species of sea turtles plus gator and crocodile noggins of all sizes. Also held the biggest sawfish bill I ever saw. Sponges, conch shells, starfish and sea fans completed the look. This was actually a pretty good collection. Only one skull I could not identify so I asked the bartender about it.

"He said it was a sea cow when it died but now, you're supposed to call them manatees. Tore him up really bad with his boat so he decided to put the poor thing out of its misery, but he was sure hard to kill without messing up the skull.

Couldn't stand to waste all that fresh meat so he towed him home, and buddy, did he eat good, better than beef and a lot more tender. Figured all that floating around keeps their muscles soft."

"Grampy, wasn't that illegal?"

"Yup, I thanked him for the information and didn't say anything at the time, but from then on, I became that place's greatest promoter. I encouraged every game warden and wildlife agent I ran into to check out that terrific little bar on Immokalee Road. The best place in the Glades to get a cold one when you are off duty and out of uniform. Don't know if I had anything to do with it, but Paradise was out of business in less than a year.

"Never was good at shooting pool but that night, since I was not fond of beer and the only sober person in the room, I was unbeatable. The winner stayed up; the loser paid for the game. I shot for free all evening.

"As the night wore on, things started getting a little rough. First there was some yelling, then shoving, and finally punching. For some reason, the guys in there that night wanted to fight and any old excuse would do! I avoided eye contact with a few of the wilder looking natives. Alcohol sure does strange things to people. When Buck informed me that he had told a friend of his at the bar that WE would gladly back him in the next brawl, I decided to run the table and leave.

"That's when Bill Fite and his wife arrived. He was a legendary cattleman, lean, hard and tanned as a Seminole. Years in the Florida sun had turned his skin to dark, wrinkled leather. He also had a paralyzed hand from a big dose of rattlesnake venom. It was frozen in a shape like he held a baseball in it. Hung at the end of his arm like a claw. The real victim was wrapped around his cowboy hat. Quite the conversation piece, that hatband.

"Mrs. Fite wasn't anything like Bill. Her skin was creamy white and flawless. She was smooth and curvy and just looked soft. Wasn't wearing any makeup except for fiery red lipstick. Her platinum blonde hair was all spun up in one of those beehives. She looked really good and way out of place. She and Bill slid into a booth, ordered a beer and watched me destroy one last cross-eyed opponent.

"When the bartender announced the approach of midnight there was a stampede for the door. Everyone except me and Mrs. Fite ran out to their trucks in order to prepare artillery for welcoming in the new year. I felt safer inside watching through the window. All I could hear was the metallic clatter of bullets and shells being jacked into every conceivable type of firearm. A regular symphony of slide actions, bolts, levers, and spinning cylinders.

"Then it got very quiet, except for the occasional huge belch. There was no fancy countdown; it would have just confused most folks anyway. Somebody finally just hollered "NOW!" and muzzle flashes lit up the whole parking lot.

"Louder than any fireworks display I've ever been to. The show wasn't all sound though, the strobe light effect of those blasts revealed some of the strangest silhouette shapes I'd ever seen. A weaving mob of contorted shadows trying to stand up and shoot at the same time.

"One fool had his arms up with a pistol in each hand, he was spinning around pulling triggers as fast as he could. Darn good thing he ran out of ammo before he fell over backwards on the pavement. He lay there cackling like a mad man and just kept pulling those triggers.

"I laughed and looked over at Mrs. Fite. She was quietly watching me. Slipped ever so gracefully out of her booth and walked straight over without blinking. Glided right through that smokey poolroom like a divine spirit through mist. Then she came in real close and gave me the look."

"All right! Finally! Um ... what look Grampy?"

"Something women perfected a million years ago. I've seen it several times and it's always the same. Done completely with the eyes. No smiling or talking involved. The whole rest of the face has a serious calmness so as to not detract from the eyes. Those eyes lock onto yours and command every cell in your body to listen closely and obey. They call to you silently and don't stop until they get what they want. Like those tractor beams they have on Star Trek, once they have you there is no escape. I was completely powerless against those eyes. She put her hand up on the back of my neck and gently guided me forward. I landed on those glowing red lips and thought my heart was going to explode. It was pounding wildly out of control, and I was having trouble getting enough air. I couldn't hear a thing anymore and forgot completely about where I was and everything else going on around us. Realized then I had kissed some girls before but never a woman. This went on for a considerable amount of time as my skill level improved quickly and even began to approach that of Mrs. Fite's.

"Not sure how long it lasted but when she finally relaxed her arms I looked up and there stood Bill Fite. And he was giving me a different kind of look. His jaw muscles were bulging out, his mouth was pulled away back on both sides and his eyes were scrunched down to slits. Scariest thing I'd ever seen in my whole life. He was trying to decide if he was going to hit me with his good hand or whack me with the claw.

"I found out later I was in more danger than I realized because Bill had been in this situation before and had done a whole lot of damage to the other guys. It was no accident that Mrs. Fite could kiss like that. She'd had a lot of practice.

"People coming back into the bar were pointing and quietly forming a circle around us. Before Bill could make up his mind, Mrs. Fite gave me a little wink, turned away and saved me by giving Bill his own New Year's kiss while dragging him back to their booth. He moved grudgingly and kept staring at me. Finally growled 'clean yourself boy, you look ridiculous.' He was referring to the gigantic smear of lipstick on my face. When he let out some half-hearted laughter, I knew it was over. The disappointed crowd sighed and staggered away shaking their heads. They wanted to see me get slaughtered!

"I grabbed some napkins off the nearest table and wiped my mouth as I was walking toward the door. I took one last look back at Mrs. Fite. She was smiling at me sheepishly and blew me another kiss as I left. That woman knew darn well I would never forget that first one, and she was right. I got out of there and never even said goodbye to Buck. He was on his own with that crowd."

"Whoa, you never cease to amaze me, Grampy, that was great! Is she the one you still think about?"

"No, Lily, don't misunderstand me, that little encounter may have been unforgettable, but it had absolutely nothing to do with love."

"Did Buck make it home all right?"

"Yup, lucky for him he did really well in a card game that evening. When he got home just before daylight, Judith was waiting by the door."

"Grampy, do you want to know what I think?"

"Sure, if it doesn't have to do with kissing. I'm tired of the subject."

"I think all these stories and jokes you tell me are supposed to teach me something without me feeling like I'm being lectured. I think you are the greatest teacher of all time."

"No, Lily, love is the greatest teacher, remember?"

"And the teacher is love."

CHAPTER ELEVEN

Star Lesson

"Oh, Lily, you tickle me so. I love you and would stay up all night talking, but old people need sleep. Look at the fire, even the flames have gone to sleep in a warm bed of coals. We'll wake them in the morning with a breakfast of fresh wood. But now it's time for sleep."

"Grampy? I can't sleep. Without the flames I'm afraid of the dark. I can't remember it ever being this dark out here before."

"All right, Lily, just one more conversation and that's it!"

Yes! I knew I could do it!

"Lily, look up and tell me what you see."

"A million billion stars."

"Anything else?"

"Yes, more stars!"

"No darkness?"

"Yeah, lots of darkness ... Oh, alright, Grampy, I get it, the stars need darkness, don't they."

"No, they don't, but you do if you want to see them. We can actually see more at night than we can during the day. Darkness isn't something to be afraid of, it's an opportunity to look beyond our own sky and see things billions of miles away. If you want to see the rest of the universe, darkness is something to look forward to. Lily, did you know that some of those stars burned out millions of years ago, technically they're dead, but their light still comes to us?"

"And they shine just as brightly as the living stars?"

"Yes, like messengers from the beginning of the universe."

"So, when the light comes to us, is that it?"

"No, little one, it keeps going."

"How far?"

"No one knows. Forever, I guess."

"Grampy, it's scary to think about that. How can anyone understand forever and endlessness?"

"Good exercise for your brain. And while you are thinking about it, don't forget that your mind can be as infinite as the universe if you want it to be."

"Grampy! If light goes on FOREVER, then that is the greatest secret! A much better one even than just getting old."

"Well, aren't you brilliant!"

"The secret is to be like a star! And shine forever, isn't it?"

"This is even making sense to me now."

"Yes! And it's love and teaching! When we teach others, our knowledge goes on for generations beyond us, maybe forever! Like light! And love is the best teacher! I've got it! I'm going to be a teacher. And I'm going to teach with love!"

"Hallelujah! Can I go to sleep now?"

"Go right ahead, Grampy, but I'm going to stay up and think about the stars . . . Grampy?"

"Yes?"

"It is so quiet."

"Except that I get the feeling you are going to keep on talking."

"The stars mean more to me now than ever."

"There is much to learn."

"Are all the answers up there?"

"Heck no, the answers are everywhere. Already forget about the sky marsh? But, hey, go ahead and look, you might discover a cure for my snoring up there."

"Maybe I can, anything is possible . . . I'm not afraid of the dark anymore."

"Just remember, Lily, you are never without starlight."

"Grampy, how can that be? What about during the day?"

"Our sun is a star, so sunlight is just a whole lot of starlight. When the earth turns away from it the other stars take over. You can trace all light back to starlight, even when it's reflected off the moon."

"Then starlight is the most important thing in the whole universe since it makes all life possible."

"Works both ways, Lily. The light certainly does make life possible, but our sun wouldn't really have any importance at all without the earth. What good is a bunch of wasted energy bouncing off God knows how many dead lifeless planets? We've been snooping around in space for quite a while and have yet to find another world with life, much less one with things like sunflowers and teenagers. The sun's very lucky to have this earth; gives it some meaning. You won't ever see me trying to get a seat on a spaceship. Living in a space station or under a bubble on the moon is my idea of pure hell. No thanks, everyone else can blast off if they want to but I'm staying right here. I love this place. And of course, I hope you stay too."

"OK, I'll stay if you keep teaching me not to be afraid."

"It's simple, Lily, the more you understand the less there is to be afraid of. We are just like the sun and the earth. What good would we be without the people we care for and nurture? They thrive in our glow and give our lives true meaning and purpose."

"OK, Mr. Sun, you're welcome. I'm proud to be your little planet. Anytime you need to beam some love and attention my way, I'll be here for you. Hey, maybe you should start planning my next birthday right now."

"HA! You are a nut!!"

"Takes one to know one, Grampy."

"Grampy, what if a great big crocodile crawls up on the beach while we are sleeping and grabs me?"

"Then I would fear your Grammy."

"Oh yeah, I wouldn't want to be you going home to Mrs. Sun without me. Boy, would she ever flare up!"

"Good grief, I have created a monster."

"Yup, all your fault. Goodnight Grampy."

"Goodnight, Swamp Lily."

Ed Carlson

CHAPTER TWELVE

Breaking Camp

I watched the stars for a long time and really did wish I could find a cure for Grampy's snoring. Only thing that could compete with him was a barred owl back on the mainland. I was glad the air was chilly. Made my sleeping bag feel warm and wonderful. I will never forget how good all over it felt to lie under the stars that night.

When I woke up, he already had the fire going and his coffee pot on the grill. He really likes his coffee and makes it the old-fashioned way by just dumping the grounds into boiling water. Says most people don't know how to make real coffee and use too much water. His stuff is really strong, and I can't even choke down a tiny sip. Told me his grampa taught him the secret to settling the grounds. You just pull that boiling tar out of the fire and sprinkle a little cold water on top. I would have to take his word for it. I'm not touching that stuff.

It really frightened me when I thought about Grampy being my age and having his own parents and grandparents. They are all gone now and if I am lucky enough to live as long as him . . . Oh no, can't even think about it. Not going to happen! I'm only going to think about right now! But maybe someday, Grampy will tell me how he handled losing the people in his life.

This was probably my favorite morning ever in the Glades. Bright sun coming up over the mangroves, crisp clear air and the world's biggest mirror to canoe in.

"Well, good morning, Lily. You look like you slept pretty well. Hear that barred owl last night? Thought I would never get to sleep with all that hoot'n."

"Trust me, Grampy, you got more sleep than me."

"Ready for breakfast? Want some coffee?"

"Yes and no."

"Come on, you're getting old, Lily. Coffee is good for you."

"That's OK. I'm fine just the way I am. I'll settle for juice."

Breakfast was biscuits and bacon. He fried the meat first in a big deep pan then removed the strips, poured out the grease, and filled it with raw dough Grammy had mixed and packed back home. With the lid on, the dough kinda fried and baked at the same time. I had my biscuits with honey and bacon on the side. Grampy tore his biscuits open and made little bacon sandwiches with gobs of ketchup. We ate sitting on the beach in our chairs, watching the Gulf.

"Not a whole lot of action this morning, Lily. Everything must be sleeping in."

"That's OK. The peacefulness is just fine."

Then off in the distance, we saw a pair of dolphins blowing and rolling their way down the shoreline slow and easy, coming up every fifty feet or so. Without any wind or wave action,

you could hear their every breath and see how smoothly their arched bodies sliced the water.

"Grampy, what is it about water that makes all the creatures in it so graceful? Things on land don't move like that, especially us."

"Prepare yourself for a shock, I do not have the answer and will not try to figure it out. A logical explanation would spoil the show."

After breakfast, I walked the beach looking for shells. Didn't find anything interesting except for some very big raccoon tracks. Is there any place these guys don't go? Talk about smart, they can figure out a way to live just about anywhere. Big old ones like this have been swimming around between these islands for years without getting caught by the gators, crocs, or sharks. Slick as that poacher Grampy knew.

By the time I got back to camp everything was packed.

"Feel like going for a cruise, Lily?"

"Absolutely!"

CHAPTER THIRTEEN

Ghosts of the Glades

Since the Gulf was smooth, we decided to take a different route back that would involve paddling "outside" the islands. Grampy thought this was a great new adventure, but I felt a little anxious about the unfamiliar route. I had to follow him this time but decided to study hard and learn this new trail forever. We stayed close to the outermost islands and were hardly ever more than a quarter mile offshore in the major passes. I had never been so far out before and felt a little nervous. Unlikely I would get clobbered by another manatee out here though, plenty of room for us to avoid collision.

There was not a single cloud in the sky and the Gulf was still calm as a puddle of oil.

"Very unusual day, Lily, this is a rare trip. There's a good river up ahead that will take us back inside. You can remember the entrance by those two sandy beaches on either side. Everything else around here is mangrove island. I'll show you a place where people lived for thousands of years."

"Anybody there now?"

"Nope, only ghosts."

"Oh great, sounds like a lovely spot."

"Don't worry, they're harmless."

We paddled into the river, riding on the incoming tide. As the channel narrowed, the current ran faster. In some quick slippery bends, we stopped paddling and just steered hard. Then it widened out again and settled down. I could see high ground and a different type of forest on the left bank. It wasn't mangroves or anything like Crescent Key. There were lots of different kinds of trees and shrubs all tangled together.

"There it is, Lily. Let's haul out on that shoreline. We will need to tie the canoes and watch them. This tide is coming up and in fast."

"Grampy, this place is as high as Crescent Key but doesn't look anything like it. There's no sand and the trees are completely different."

"That's because it's a pile of Native American garbage, covered by plants they grew for food and medicinal purposes."

"Wow, this is a lot of garbage."

"Not really, considering how many people lived here and dumped the shells of oysters, conchs, clams, and other species that they had eaten for thousands of years. Not to mention the bones of the many reptiles and mammals they ate. This seems like a nice tidy place to me. Especially without all the bottles, cans, plastic, and appliances we pile up to the sky nowadays. These Indian mounds made great, fertile home sites."

"What happened to these people, Grampy?"

"Lily, a culture that was doing just fine even before the Egyptian pyramids were built was wiped out by diseases brought by European explorers and settlers just a few hundred years ago. Imagine people living here for thousands of years thinking life would go on as usual forever. Now they are gone without a trace except for this pile of shells and bones."

"It is spooky, Grampy. Think of all the families and their stories. They had dreams and all the same feelings we do. Those kids had canoes and Grampies and went fishing too. Maybe we can't be like stars and shine forever."

"Lily, history is full of eternal stars. These people were as smart as us and I am sure there were great inspiring teachers and philosophers in this culture. But what they didn't have was a written language to carry the wisdom forward and they could have never dreamed that a biological disaster would wipe them out."

"We do know from the written accounts of the earliest explorers that these were huge people and fierce warriors. Seven-foot-tall men were common, and their bows were so powerful the Spanish soldiers couldn't even pull them back. These people could shoot an arrow right through European armor. Ponce de León stuck his flag on Florida's east coast without a problem but when he tried it over here, got himself shot and killed."

"Wow, Grampy, all that strength and courage destroyed by germs?"

"Yup, Lily, it's a good lesson for us to remember. The best military in the world can't defeat the forces of nature. In fact, it's the other way around."

"Grampy, what's that funky smell? Could there be a skunk up here?"

"It's possible but I think what you are smelling are some of these tropical plants. Probably the camphor trees and stopper shrubs. Indians used them to treat all kinds of ailments. These gumbo limbos, cocoplums, and strangler figs were also useful. But there is one thing I know they weren't good for."

"What's that?"

"Repelling mosquitos! They're as fierce in here as the old Indian warriors and have arrows for noses. Let's get back on the water!"

Pulling away from the Indian mound, I felt so sad that whole civilizations can just disappear. I mean, what was the point? Could the same thing happen to us? Aren't we supposed to be doing all this learning and growing and building for some purpose? Are we really just doing all this to pass the time?

"Lily, why the serious look?"

"That place made me sad, Grampy. It felt like a graveyard for people and their dreams."

"Lily, I think you are right. Some of our greatest lessons are difficult to accept and sometimes even depressing. But it is still important to learn them and shape our lives by understanding them. That Indian mound taught me something very important."

"What?"

"That time and change never stop. Always seemed to me like time has two speeds. The slow steady here and now when nothing seems to be changing, and the unlimited speed you can achieve with your imagination. With a good imagination you can go backward or forward through time as far and as fast as you want. I always found it easier to think about the past, and more difficult, even frightening sometimes, to imagine the future. Most future changes are good, but some are not, like losing those whom we love very much. However, if you have the courage to think about the future and all its possibilities, good and bad, you will be able to accomplish more positive things and anticipate and accept the hard changes more easily."

"OK, Grampy, if you say so, I'll try."

Well, there it was, the lesson about loss. I knew he would do it. Slipped it in like a net under a trout. Never dreamed we would go through Indians and lost cultures to get there. I promised myself to think about the future a lot, even if it hurt.

We followed that little river quietly from then on. I didn't know what Grampy was thinking about, but my thoughts were flying from the beauty of the Glades that day to my future as a teacher and life as an adult. We didn't say anything when we met the old trail home and Grampy let me take the lead. No need, there was so much to think about.

Ed Carlson

Acknowledgements
for editorial comments
thanks to:

Jo Ann Carlson and Amelia McCarty

Beth Preddy

Stuart McIver

Linda and Amy Stetson

Illustrations:

Jo Ann Carlson

Mary Bartrop

www.ingramcontent.com/pod-product-compliance
Lightning Source LLC
Chambersburg PA
CBHW070745280626
47162CB00017B/2358